The Musings of an Old Wizard

From the Tales of Olorin

Other translated scrolls
Of the Tales of Olórin

Filtered down through the stars
Wind in the trees
The transcending song
The blue wizards
Secret fire
Bend in the road
Ever on goes the road

"In the beginning Eru, the one, who in the Elvish toung is named

Iluvatar

J.R.R. Tolkien

To whom this volume is dedicated to

gons
les
N
W
E
S
do
Re
m
on
ndo
The River Kings
DRAG
BE

ELVES CAVE
Home of Ladsfriend
DWARFS
S
RE
The druin
Mtt
2008

"Involved"

It is often said that one should not get involved in the affairs of wizards and dragons… but it is seldom remembered and not widely known that wizards start out their journeys with the memories of young boys; I won't even talk about dragons here. Boys are told this over and over, and yet some boys do find themselves "Involved". Some by choice, some by chance, fancy, or fate. Are you chosen to be a wizard, or do you choose to be one? If chosen, then not by those who warn us to not get "involved," If we choose, then it's not perceived as a very wise course of action, to say the least…

I have come to know that names and the names that places are called become relevant only to their own times by perspective or when joined by some great evil that forever keeps them bound, those are best left unspoken if remembered. So, I have decided to leave them out of my memoirs to protect myself from any such evil and to keep tarnish away from others that may or may not be associated with the events described. I leave out dates, keeping only to the telling of the tales, leaving the quibblers to argue the colors of the ink and the strokes of my pen. There are a few names that span the whole of time and those are known, or shall be made known to all, in time: from time to time. And many of those will be made clear whether seen on the horizon or gleaned from some old dusty manuscripts. "Many" is the word that only leaves you guessing, guessing about a thing you really ought to know. Now then, sirs, let's not miss the mystery of the lesson from the lady's dim reflection or catch a dirk in the back while marking a map.

Oh my dear were to begin? So many things I try to remember and so many I wish that I could forget. So I suppose I should begin with:

Once there was a boy named Lad... Lad was not his Proper or a birth name and he would have many names as time passes; but like I said, before, names will be left in the misty grey past. Suffer my old bones for the sake of my tale to call him Lad. I submit that to call him a boy would not be quite fare at this point in time in the telling he was more of a sapling of a man. A very young man with a strong will and lots of questions about well, just about everything. As most younglings, Lad had a position in life, a charge as it were, and all the things that came of it, wardrobe, a good horse and saddle, a hat, sword, lamp and a message bag. He was known from edge-land to edge-land as the Wanderer or the Rover for he was always wandering around matching a message with a face or a package with a place, always being warned not to go too far or get involved; just deliver the message or package and ride on....

At first, it was easy not to become involved but the more he would think about how much the contents of what he delivered or imparted would change the lives of the people and the places that he would "visit," the harder it was to not be involved, to stay nameless, faceless; just do the deed and move along to the next. Lad was never paid for his services in the coin of the realm, but he was always fed and offered lodging. His druthers, however, was to hunt and sleep outside. He had become quite the woodsman, tracker, and horseman besides. Lad came to know the forest creatures as friends. Some of such was his lifelong friend and his friends beautiful bride. They were building a home down by the river. Unlike the village people they worked and loved all of nature and all of nature in turn loved and worked with them. Even in song and dance birds and critters came from miles around And OH could his wife sing. All and all his lifelong friend was a man like any, other putting on his pants one leg at a time. Only when he put his pants on, he put on his gold boots as well.

Lad spent allot of his time on the river with his lifelong friend, listening to his tales and fishing its banks. His friend often spoke as one who actually lived through the times he spoke of. Not just tale casting some old stories. You know the ones told as generations hand them down from fireplace to campfire, or from the dinning halls of great fallen kings. His eyes would sparkle as he would laugh at the falling of a great fire worm or well up with tears as he spoke in hushed reverent tones of the decreasing encounters with the woodland folk who moved like the wind; seldom spoke of or seen by village dwellers but, no! They were not spirits of the mists they had their own legacy and histories of

old yes even older than man's. It was during one of his stories that my lifelong friend told me " Soon it would be that I would meet with them".... Not many days later.

The sparks and brands of the fire startled me to full alertness. I jumped to my feet, sword in hand. I scanned the camp and at first all seemed well.... Slowly I could just make out the fire's reflection in a pair of eyes from deep in the woods from across the glowing flames. How long was I dozing off? Just staring? And how long were the eyes in the dark staring at me? No sounds except the crackle of heat in the wood; the air was still with no wind or strange scent. The horses were calm and did not feel the robed figure that was walking toward me.

"How fare you, stranger" I called out to the form, without fear or hesitation a hail shot back:

"In good spirits but with no time for chit chat or small talk of weather or fishing spots"!!!

I don't know what startled me the most; was it the clarity of the voice or the dawning awareness that it Was a woman that responded with such calm boldness!

Was she alone? Just then, the horses scuffed and neighed, jumped around as if woken from a sleep just as I was from my own thoughts. She moved swiftly and with confidence, toward me and around the fire ...

" Might I sit and warm myself a spell?" she asked; Now I was staring face to face with incredible beauty; durable yet soft, strong with youthful vigor. Slender and as a tall child in stature, graceful-necked, she had silver flowing tresses these were offset by a small nose and remarkable ears that seemed, well like that of a fox, not covered with fur or folded over but ending in a most delicate tip. Her stance was sturdy and under her cloak, she was clad in the colors of the forest. She wore a short sword in sheath and a slung bow of white that did not reflect the firelight. I don't know how long I stared into her eyes searching for what—a reason? A response? Even in the light of the fire, I could see they were green. Suddenly she sat down spryly on her heels, ready to spring if need be... "I was warned that your folk were slow and dull of senses," she said while pushing back her hair. "So I will speak with common words and give you plenty of time to respond." I broke out in full laughter and said "No, no, it's not that. You are quite quick and stealthy; it's your manner of appearance that has overwhelmed me, as if by an enchantment, even my four-legged companions were taken unaware. Mostly, it is your strange raw beauty that has left me without speech just now." She lowered her gaze to the fire and said, "Well spoken, friend. There seems to be no fear or malice in your hail or hospitality, although it is lacking in food or ale in the offer." "I, fair lady, have both bread and sweet wine and you are welcome to your fill." She smiled. I looked at her and drank her in. "Are you alone?" I asked. "In the dark? In the woods?" It was her turn to laugh. Smoothly, she swung her arms wide. "I am never alone or in the dark. I am here to give you a scroll that you shall deliver to the Kings of the River.

It is sealed and must go to them at first light. You are the one called the Wanderer or the Rover, are you not?" Yes, I am called that, although my friends call me Lad." Then, Wanderer, I will call you Lad. I am called the Whisper in the Trees. You will call me Witt, as my friends call me. Now let's be about that bread and wine.

The morning was darker than most. The sun was not yet up, and there was no telling how the fire stayed burning so long into the night, maybe due to some craft of Witt. After the wine that night we came close for the heat and the comfort; she had plenty of both with a playful willingness to share. We slept in each other's arms under the stars in the clearing of the trees by the brook. When I was fully awake, she was gone. I could tell that when she left, she took my heart; alas, in its place on the message bag by the saddle was the scroll. It was then that I heard the songbird singing and knew it was time I was on my way. Strange letters were embossed on the cuff of the scroll around the back side of the seal that I had not seen before but now somehow were glowing in the pre-dawn darkness. I could reason in all the dialects of the edge-lands but these I had not seen; I would have to show these to and ask my lifelong friend about the Kings of the river and how to find them.

Scores of birds flew around her as she sang with boldness and warmth swirling on the wind like the smell of fresh baked bread; it was a joy to hear and watch her from up on the bank. As I walked down the hill to the River, I could see my lifelong friend was fishing with a net, his wet hat dripping down in his face onto his full dark beard. I stood still and took in the sight, the smell, the beauty; as much as any place this was home to me, as I wandered over the hills and far away...

"The River Kings?" "That's a sour group to dance with! Lad, are you sure this 'Witt' was not some fancy born of too much of my blackberry wine?"

I went eye to eye with my friend and said, "I would

have thought so myself if not for the scroll and the lingering of her scent on my clothes."

"Ah, the birds say the story is true enough," chimed in the Lady of the river. "Witt is just now leaving the land that you call edge-land. She has met with a group of her own and taken to the mountains of mist; they move fast because they are being pursued."

"Pursued!" I yelled "By what or whom? Are they in danger?"

The lady did not lose her calmness as she responded to me, "No, the only danger would be to those who pursue, should they catch them up. On the trail the wood folk are great warriors as well as lovers." She smiled. "The birds have other stories as well. The owl tells of long embraces in the night: but I see no harm has come to you...Witt lingered long watching you sleep before leaving in the early darkness this day. She is older than most trees but younger than the hills; she is spry and chose well from man-lings. I have asked my feathered fiends not to give word to her kin as they have done for me; not all understand the ways of young love..." I felt my face turn red as my heart pounded like a blacksmith's anvil as the hammer of what she said rang threw my mind. Trying to gather my composure, I asked her, "The birds see all these things?" "Oh yes, and more. The deer can smell her scent on you as well. The convergence of edglings and wood-ling surprises and delights them. You are a wonder to them; even now they are calling you a young wizard." "Who are they?" I ventured.

"Why, the creatures of the forest!" She sang and danced around as if giving us and them her blessing. "They have gone off to tell the wizard of the trees of you, in hope that he will teach you what he knows of the old ones, their ways, and of the symbols that they used in days long past. But enough of that, you must be off to the river to deliver the scroll. It is of great import to the Kings of the river." The river ran small at that point but opened up into a much greater waterway farther down. I made haste. The Lady had assured me she would watch my horses and that her boat would guide me. My lifelong friend shrugged and smiled, waving toward the boat that he had been filling with fresh provisions. As I pushed off the shore, I could see that there were fish, a blanket and clothing much like the wood-colored cloth that Witt had worn; there was even a small, sturdy sword in a sheath like the one she wore around her waist. On the off chance I sniffed, but it did not smell like her. As the boat took me down the river, my thumb was rubbing over the green jewel set in the hilt of the short sword. It felt harder than the steal it was set in yet was warm in the sunlight. Somehow it reminded me of her... Beautiful and exotic, hard and sharp, yet warm and comforting in my hands... Suddenly something overhead caught my eye: Eagles. Two ahead of me, one over top, and three behind me. They seemed to be watching me as they soared and rose on the thermals from the high-reaching banks of the river. This is where the river widened out with Tall broken spires of a lost empire reaching into the clear sky on both sides of the river. The trees around this place, although large and old, were dead and grey. Not burned by fire, but dried out, as if their roots had been cut off under the earth.

The Eagles dove in low around the trees and landed in a circle on the stone dock work along the river. The water looked black. In its depths the boat moved out over the current and came to a stop there in front of the six Eagles.

Eagles.... see it all and yet can tell few, even if others could understand. The risk of trying to approach them was so dangerous and filled with fear; trying to communicate, so tedious, slow, Eagles use a lot of eye movement, pupal dilation, and scratching of their talons. Lost on so many races of men that have no skill or patience for them. A ways back I learned from an eagle that I had come across, It was shot by a *dart and close to death; I cared for and fed it, back to full strength so He could fly again . This eagle would keep coming back to stare at me right into my eyes it was unnerving, but I finally figured out that he was communicating with me. I wanted to fly with him; of course, I could not so I danced instead and he would fly beside me as I danced with my arms outstretched soaring on the ground with my new eagle friend as he flew up and over and around me; for days we winded and twirled until my energy was drained to the ground and blown away to the wind. My new friend stood over me as I slept, I could hear his talons scratching out the tales of his fathers and their promise to protect the sons of men, and his promise to do the same for me. In the high sun of the next day, he picked me up in his talons and set out for the mountain peaks. Never had I dreamed of such wonder; I had no fear and could see far and wide. This time I was really soaring above river, stone, and trees, up to a high peek he took me to where an old lookout tower had been built long ago, the tower had a long set of stone stairs set in the wall of the mountain. He told me that it was an important place for my kind in days gone by and that it had had many names given to it by man and elf and dwarf none that I shall name here. We watched the sun sink low on the horizon of night together in a solemn quietness, listening to the wind below us in the canyons. Then he looked at me, spread his mighty wings and without so much as a flutter, lifted into the wind and soared straight into the orange globe. I sat there, absorbing the moment until the cold and dark sent me to explore the tower for shelter and new adventures. I've seen him a few times, seance and he has always remembered me, reporting many things going on afar off that could and did have great effect on my life, and many more that would come about in times ahead...... like now like here on the shore of this lost and lonely palace.

* Wounded by an arrow

The Eagles stood there in a circle, calmly watching me as I tied off the boat. I called to them as I walked over, scroll in hand "Are you the river Kings?" ...no reply...only the sound of talons on stone as they shifted, looking again at me and shifting their heads they took turns to fly off. circling higher and higher then away to the north from where they came. Understanding now the warning I looked Behind me. I became aware of flaming torches set in sconces deep in the receding halls of the ruins. I set my nerve. unsheathed the blade and made my way in, blade in one hand scroll in the other. My footsteps were like drums in the deep darkness of the chamber; it was as if a sound had never been made in this place. Slowly a blue glow began growing before me as the chamber opened into a great hall. The walls were marked and clawed, and everything was chard by fire the very air was thick with a sulfur brim. In the dim light I could see a great blue stone giving off a pale glimmer. Perched on both sides of the gem were giant snake-like creatures with wings and faces that looked a bit; like cats, coiled on and around gold coins, jewels, bones, and ancient weapons. I could see their glowing eyes watching me through heavy half-open lids. The eyes of the dragons shown in the cloudy reflection on the floor like smoke on the water. A loud clear hissing voice broke the silence like glass. "Who has come to wake the kings of the river" I could not tell who spoke. My mind screamed that it could not be one of the serpents before me, but my heart could feel else wise. clearing my mind and my thoughts I replied I am but a messenger and have come to bring a scroll to the river kings from the wood-folks of the mountains of mist; if you would show me to these Kings then I will be on my way. Horrible Hideous laughter broke from both sides of the blue gem the heads of the creatures came around as one to face me. are we not royal enough for you man-ling? do you see us as mere watchdogs for some higher court? spoke the dragon on the left .... " Let us burn and eat this fool before he speaks again" spoke the other. If you burn me, you will not be able to read the scroll; My Sires it is your pardon I beg not being accustomed to such power in my short lifetime. (More hideous laughter... this time lauder.) "Why should we not end your short life or even care to read the scroll of a people that perished into history, them and their sons wandering like leaves before the winds, forgotten as you... soon will be?"

Well now because you are Great kings that value knowledge and the worth of time and as not to squander any more of yours, I will leave this scroll on the dock just outside the main doorway and you shall never know that I have come and gone. This time there was no laughter, only a deep growl that might have been compliance or even agreement, I did not wait I turned hoping against hope that their curiosity would not allow them to burn me while I was holding the scroll. I fingered the gem with my thumb again as I held on to the hilt of the elvish sword. in my other hand, I grasped the scroll moving swiftly and steady down the hall. I got about three steps before one of the dragons ran along the ceiling above me and jumped down in front of me blocking my way.

My mind was staggered by its lightning agility as it wrapped its tail around my legs and plucked the scroll from my hand... "Not so fast Rover, do you think we have not heard of you or know of your coming? we are after all Kings of this realm nothing moves through or over us without our leave not even the great eagles or the fair ladies' boat...So why should we not burn and eat you... Now that the scroll is safe within our grasp?"

Sir that I may return your reply after you have read the message that has been sent to you? Another growl from behind as the second dragon sniffed at my hat a fair request for a messenger to own free passage. why such boldness and risk for one who has no involvement with dragons prior to this day? Upon coming here, I knew not that dragons would be connected

Only kings and kings can and should be trusted; the greater the king the greater the trust; besides any tyrant can take a life only a great king can grant one.

(I had come to learn much later in life that however true the information or words of a dragon; spoken or passed along, their intention or motivation is always evil, or somehow always shrouded in lies that speak death to the spirit behind them.)

The first dragon almost made a purring sound as he dropped me from his grip. The size of the dragons seemed to shrink and swell to their needs one moment twice their size the next only slightly bigger than a horse with wings. The second dragon moved to face the other it was then than that I saw that he had an eye of a different color the first dragon had two yellow eyes and the second dragon had one yellow eye and one green eye. The first dragon spoke, "It seems we have been bested by our own honor brother. Perhaps sparring this rover could be a message in itself that we will listen to the wood-folk again..." the green-eyed dragon slowly responded, "Or maybe his disappearance would be a greater message that we are done with them and their kind forever." Now I did not know the ways of dragons or to this point in time think them to even be real outside of stories meant to scare children. Dragons were Imaginings of those who had lost their way and their wits; the core of drunken stories spoken when too much ale was spilled in taverns late at night. but in all my days since I have never heard of a dragon to ever return something that he had taken away from anyone but that is what happened next. The dragon with both yellow eyes

handed me back my sword and said "Tell them we will read the scroll" Hissing echoed in the darkness. "Do not return to us mangling! for we shall give no quarter" Moving toward the door in the great chamber, I remembered the letters and symbols on the stone that held up the blue gem, they stood out to me only because I had seen them on the scroll for the first time! could the dragons talk was strange enough for me but read as well? as I fled the hall into the light of day what stood out in my mind the most was the green-eyed dragon, I could not help but wonder if each dragon thought he looked like the other, as in a mirror for in fact the resemblance was remarkable. Did one think they both had yellow eyes,

and the other think they both had one yellow and one green eye, or did they know the difference between them. It also did not escape me how that green eye reminded me of the gemstone on the hilt of the short sword that I was staring into just now...

The light on my skin felt as the warmth of life itself after coming out of the darkness under the mountains. I don't know if the glare of the yellow eyes will ever leave my nightmares and dark dreams; somehow, they held me captive more than my physical movements at the time. I splashed clean, cold river water into my face, and shook off the smoke from my hair, breathing deep of the clear late-day air. The sun was going down on me in a strange place. As I got back into the boat; it was gliding upstream against the current. I changed into the wood-ling cloths pondering such a craft that without a paddle, moved up the river over the black waters deep underneath me. Soon sleep overtook me as I listened to its song.

The march was long and hard, and the wood-folk moved like shadows along it. Most folk to this day are not aware of dragon lore and this small bit has proved to be very interesting to me. I found it carved in a stone high on a cliff perhaps, long before the most of us were on this earth maybe by a boastful dragon himself keeping in mind their propensity for lies. But it went something like this: Dragons breath fire so that they can fly above the layer of air (who else but a dragon would know this) higher than the mountains they don't need air, they can see the smallest things on the ground like the eagles only much better it is from this position that they must have surveyed the land and what was going on below seeing the wood-folk walk back into the forest. In the years of man-folk, Witt was 2000 springs of age; very young for her people to be out and about on a mission of such great import, yet she had proven herself a very skillful scout and craftswoman, none could speak to the birds or the other animals as effectively as she could and she spent all of her time in the woods, she was not a dell dweller she would much rather sleep under an apple tree and usually did. She loved green apples; She loved everything green! Just as Witts company went into the trees of the forest she could feel the eyes of a great evil upon them from far off but she could not glean from ware; the mountains were hidden behind the trees and the sky was clear to her keen eyes yet... "What is troubling you lass spoke OAK-HELM he was the leader of this party" you seem ill at ease" "We are watched from some great distance my Lord but I can not tell it" "HMM must be some craft of the old ones or a dragon perhaps, not to worry we are home now and covered by the branches of friends; a song erupted by the troupe as they got closer to the dell and hearts became lighter. Oak-helm was a great singer he actually was good at everything that he did, and he especially loved to sing; the birds joined in, and the other animals gathered close...

"Friends like branches reach from the tree

With roots long and strong as family

deep in the ground like our ancestral land brings

life and all things good to our hand"

.... To glide along and listen to the wood-folks song. Tonight, there would be grand fires, ale, and new stories told, everyone was filled with hope thinking that the winged worms would help them to rid the cave of stones from the fire dweller... Not just any stones by any means the stones in this cave were colored and translucent they gave a radiance and light some cold to the touch and some warm or hot. Some were as bright as starlight in the darkness and always a source of power and trade for the wood-folk. No one knows where the old one came from some were calling it a fire dweller or one of the ancient evil elders that left the path of light, and strayed from the righteous ones, the teachers of the songs. Maybe he awoke from deep back in the cave itself but over the last two springs, it had fortified the front of the cave and kept everyone out. Seldom was it seen outside and only for a short while some say that the stones are his food or rather the energy that they give off and there is plenty of water in the cave, (if a fire beast even needs water) no attempt to reason with it gave any fruit. Swift and sudden death came to those who ventured too close. Sometimes I can't remember all of the tale and who told me what part of the telling they blend together, like an afternoon dream and being older than snow makes it hard sometimes, but as I recall it was Witt that told me this at this leg of the journey that these things be true...

I could hear squalling from the water down below, so I moved toward the sound along the bank of the river, a scruffy little critter was caught in a fast-moving current for a long time. The cold water began to draw out its life; finally, the power of the river forced it up onto a clutch of branches collecting from the side ... I don't know how long it had been there clinging for its life when I heard its little yelping sounds. After pulling it to safety, I gave it a good look over, it was a wolf cub with its front paw injured and the left eye was swollen shut, maybe lost. I saw it was a male and small enough to fit in my hand, I didn't know how young but not yet weaned, there was no way I would let the river take it. I decided to bring him to the lady of the river, knowing she could fix him up right quick if I could get him there alive and in time. I tucked him into a fold of my cloak to keep him warm and dry... The little fur-ball went to sleep. The wind came up, and with it, the first snow. There were still leaves on the trees, most showing brilliant colors of the early fall. These were ripped and shredded from their branches, even the creatures of the woods were caught off guard by this.... storm? Strange sounds like shrieking voices could be heard on the gale, not of man or animal. I was feeling very fortunate of all the provisions that the wood folk had packed me with - warmer clothes and a cloak as well plenty of food and a quiver full of their arrows; the best I'd ever seen. They shot like smooth moss over wet stone and the rugged bow was easy to draw back. The harsh sound now in my ears had not quite blocked out the memory of the music and fellowship of the past few suns spent with Witt and her people. The trail was getting covered by the snow as it fell heavily even in the strong wind, it stuck to the ground like it had its own will to stay. Darkness came fast already I yearned for the crimson glow of the next sunrise. The moon shining through the quick-moving clouds shone on the ice that clung to the sides of the trees and rocks.

It also shone in the steam of thunder's breath and gleamed in his eyes. It was time to seek shelter from the storm. Up ahead was a light on the horizon. This was my seventeenth winter, and the most sudden storm I had ever seen one come on, and my first one out alone. I was not ready for the darkness. I was longing for the sun gone afar off in the west and for the people of the flowers that dwelt there. Was there a land of perpetual summer, as the songs told? Was it real or just a myth to keep hope alive on the coldest, darkest winter nights? My thoughts were getting too heavy. I brushed my hand against the wolf pup to check him. There was some warmth there, my eyes began to tear up and swell, maybe it was the sting of the cold and driving snow, there was a strange comfort from the warm little yelper. My own warmth was draining as I reached the home of my friend. A door opened to me.... the last thing I saw before sleep took me was his face outlined by the warm glow of the fire. There's a feeling I get when I look to the west, when my spirit is crying for leaving. Voices call me from that coast, I know that a time is coming that I will be heading out that way. Sometimes everything around me becomes a distraction for my thoughts, and other times I can't soak enough in to capture it, embrace it, forever to hide it away someplace to save and visit it whenever I need to. As it was, then again it will be. sometimes the flow may change but rivers always reach the sea. I was in such a time as this... I could feel the power surge through me into my core and back out like new breath flowing and growing, Joy unspeakable and full of glory vibrating my whole being. I could call to the wind, and the wind would answer me and teach me things that I did not yet know. I wanted to share this with the whole world or anyone who would listen. Was there ever a time when I could look back and see a flow that took me to where I was now? I slip and slide in and out of my own memories. Who am I and where am I from?

I have knowledge from longer back than I should, at least that is what my head tells me. Ages passed as though I was there, things I know of peoples long gone, wars over places that no longer have names. Lands that have gone beneath the waves of the seas. The very scape of the land has changed now, leaving my recollections dazed and confusing, never coming into focus. So, I try not to spend too much time putting it all together; everything moves around too much. Like a dark spire on the distant horizon, obscured by clouds and waning light of the moon... Kind of makes me feel sometimes like I just don't want to grow, but as the eagle leaves the nest I've got so far to go. Just then, I could smell smoke in the air, so I climbed the ridge to get a good look around. From a higher vantage point, I could see on one ridge the wind was filled with the sound from the forest below; calm, quiet, I saw the fire over the other side. Men and horses around it, not quite a hunting party, more like a small army. They moved about the camp with purpose, and all were dressed the same from boot to helm, even the horses were the same in color with the saddle and leather bindings. With no shining steal, everything was dark so it would not reflect the sun. The men were very quiet as they moved about and spoke in low tones, with no fast motions, nothing but the smoke of the fire called any attention to them. I could now see several small fires that began to glow in the falling darkness.

I made my way back down to my horse that I called by the name of Thunder. We disappeared into the trees, my little pup was all but grown and doing well, he would come and go from me during the day as he hunted for himself and then catch me up in the eve. He would stay till early morn and usually be gone before I broke camp. As small as he started out in this life, he was now massive in size, with a shiny bright coat with bright blue eyes, the one that was damaged healed well due to the lady of the river. She told me that one day he might take off back to the ways of his kind but would never forget the favor shown him. I never gave him a name; he just never needed one. Somehow, we could read each other's thoughts. Thunder and the wolf got along great from the start and worked well together, giving each other the space that they needed. We rode long into the night, putting the camp of the men leagues behind us. We rode all that night and the next two nights. We went without a fire and ate from our dried stores, well except the wolf he just cocked his head and watched me over a fresh rabbit. That night I remembered, as I fell asleep, thinking about our destination of the castle of the river kings, and I shuddered. Hearing the voice in the back of my mind, "Do not return to us man-ling"....

Again my heart yearned for the music of the wood folk and for time spent with Witt I longed to hear her sing with me and to watch the wonderment dance in her eyes. Her people had their own stories told in the song that had taught me much and still this hunger burned within me for more; sometimes I would sit at the base of a water fall close as I could get just to absorb the wonderful power that billowed and churned even in its random falling, I could feel its pattern as I reeled to the rhythm it gave me strength from the inside out, flowing like the river that created it. Sometimes giant logs would come crashing, splintering down exploding all around me. Thunder and the wolf would watch from up on a ridge exchanging glances that questioned my wisdom. Our little troupe skirted the towns as much as possible but when we did have to venture into one, we stuck close together. Thunder and his closeness to the wolf raised allot of eyebrows; people would move wide around them as they noticed he was sitting there; I had fastened a small pack to his upper back. that held a sharp blade and a few other things he could bring to me in a pinch nevertheless he looked as wild as he was. When Witt met him, it was love at first glance I was watching woulph watching Witt for the longest time He did not take his eyes off her all night except to look over to me in approval and affection.

Witt would move in and stroke his thick fur. It made me glad that their bond was close. there were times when woulph would escort her back to her own woods sometimes staying gone for days at a time giving her extra safety even though she was a formidable foe to many.

I spent a lot of time just sitting and thinking, drawing from my pipe as the sun and moon moved over me, causing my shadow to go around and around and around. It was as though I became a part of the place I sat for a time, soaking in the smells the sounds, learning and growing, listening to the birds as they would tattle on the rest of their brothers and sisters. I would wonder what it was that held all things to together and why some things were just not moving in the flow with the rest; wayward, restless, lost, displaced. Many times, I've wondered how much there is to know. the long-extended summer ended overnight. leaves are fallen all around its time I was on my way following this rocky ridge the gleaner's moon lights my way. Strange tales were told about creatures that walked here, those that shunned the day and hunted in the moonlit pools below in the river; creatures changed by the darkness itself; folk who wandered for too long or too far back into the dark hills and mountain mines, looking for something that drew them in and found them, or some part of there soul that they could not relinquish, keeping them ever bound to the shadow realm. I wondered if that is what was hounding my every step now. I could hear it and caught a few glimpses of it threw the trees. It was a bit more stealthy on the rocks, but I could hear its pad like shuffle. Was it curious or purposeful? Hand to hilt, I moved against the wall of the cliff face, away from the trail to allow it passage so I could get a good look at it. The stone in the hilt of my sword brushed my hand... taking my eyes from the task. Its green brilliance reminded me of witts eyes as they sparkled in the firelight; it seemed like so long ago... The beautiful woman stared as she walked by and took me in view, hat and all; the clothes of a wanderer. I wondered what she thought she saw.

I never thought I would end up an old man writing in taverns, telling tales of youth gone by and loves that came and went, burned up and blown away like a dry leaf. HMMMmmm There may be a few adventures left in me still. Now where was I? Oh yes, the creature; moving along the pass behind me. It stopped to listen, it waited a long time before venturing forward in my direction as it came around the bend, I could see its greenish-yellow eyes, very large for its head size. The full moon was mirrored in both of them as they scanned past me along the rock face. It was then that I saw the shadow reflected there in this hapless imp's eyes as it moved across the moon, reflected there I slowly looked up and watched it fly in front of the cold, full face of the moon one more time. It was not a dragon but something darker, an even older evil that was searching, ever searching..... my blood went cold, and the little creature that was

Woulph

on the path scampered off into the darkness. It was in full, fearful fright for its life, no longer trying to be silent but running headlong, splashing into the river below. I found a ledge out of the wind and watched for the winged creature again. I lit the bowl of my burl pipe that I kept in a fold of my cloak, letting the smoke blow freely. I found it calming and helped me gather my thoughts to sit and pull on that old pipe. I lost it many years (latter)or should I say (ago) in a fall deep in a mine; a mine can be a dangerous place. That was not to be my only encounter with a mine, As I sat blowing rings of smoke threw my knees, my eye was drawn to a smooth part of the rock face. To my astonishment, it was glowing in the moonlight. A symbol was carved just under the moss. I brushed it away and felt for deep groves but only found a smother inlay... now I had come this way many a day and not a few nights, and never have I seen a trace of this glowing rune before, albeit I don't remember coming at moonlight. The symbol was simple yet had a tangible power. Two elongated circles intertwined with five points. The points were stones; the two outside stones and the one in the middle were like starlight, the other two set inside the circles were blood red. I just stared in wonderment with no idea as to what I was looking at. The whole idea was older than time; was it a map or the marker of some bygone kingdom, perhaps a warning? I looked around for other indications or clues, in this small quest I found a long straight tree branch leaning in the back corner out of the way of view to anyone going by in any direction. it was a well-seasoned walking staff of sorts with a crystal intertwined in the roots of one end; it suited my needs to clear duff from the corners of my newly found nook.

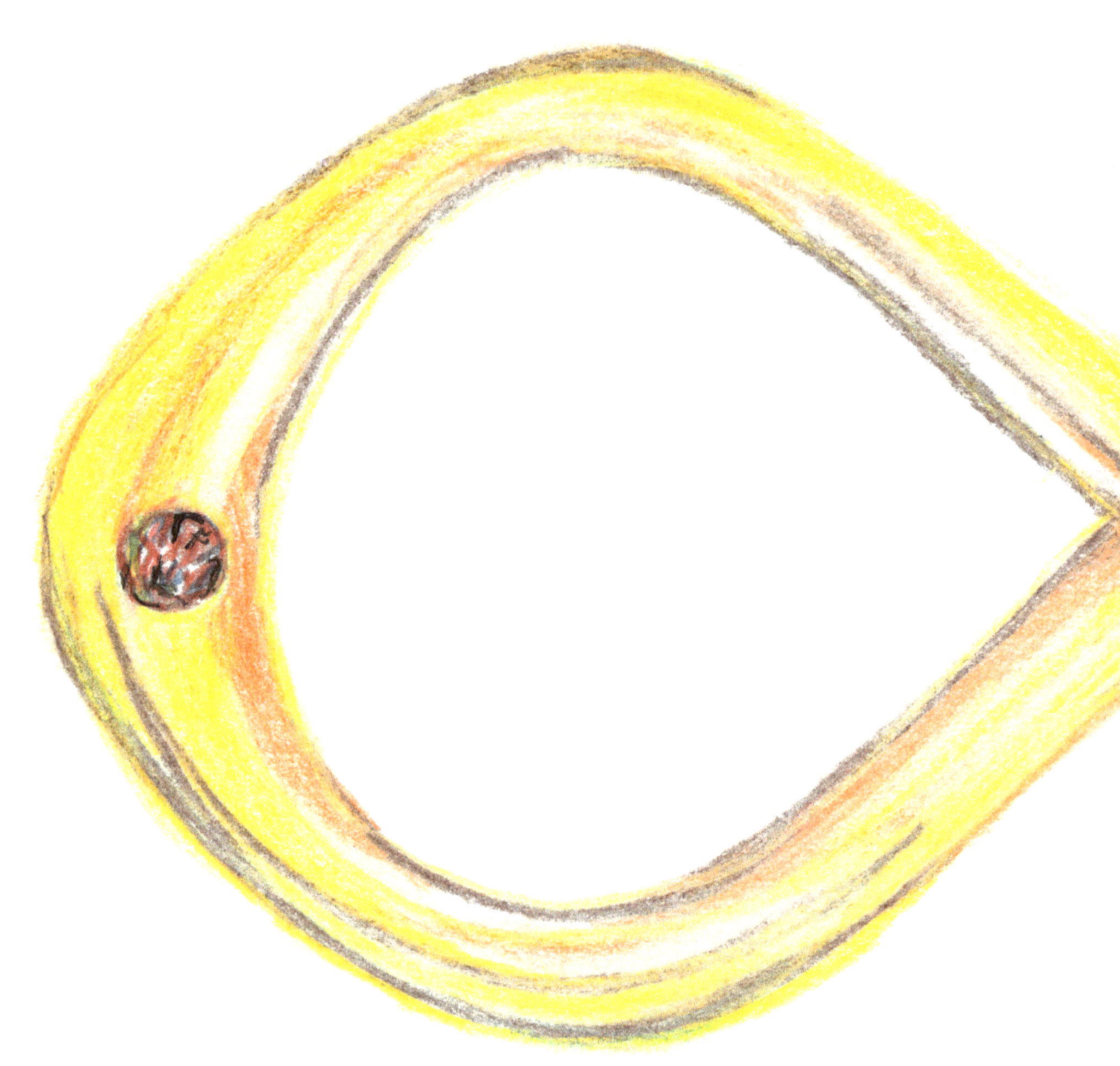

As I dug along the ledge close to the edge with the staff that I found, I could hear music and voices that seemed to come from inside the mountain itself. Songs with many voices and much emotions... I sat and listened in wonderment; the songs seemed to comfort and teach all at the same time. The sounds came through the rock face that was in front of me... I did not want to leave, so I stayed for hours and hours. I learned of days gone by, I found that if I came at the same moon phase, I would find the same. I longed to meet them or at least to see them. Who could they be? After a few visits to the ledge, I realized I could understand their tung and found myself singing the songs as I went my way down the lonely road. Sometimes the seasons go by so fast, and others they seem to stand still, this was that time... when I would sit there on the ledge and listen, learn languages and histories, tales of Wars and swords, powers that have come and gone, whole ages that are only found in the rubble of ruins overgrown with trees and crumbled into fields were the foxes and owls are living in the halls of fallen kings. This is where I learned of ships that sailed out on the open waters of the seas and the deserts.

In the songs, i learned of the one called the creator from before the stones of power the dwellers of the houses of the holy the fall of the evil one that once was pure that hunted the stones he hungered for. Creatures born in the dark depths that feed on human flesh and even each other.

I learned of ships and the ocean; strange beings of the seas Lands of ice and snow the midnight sun where the hot springs grow and sand with blowing dust all these things i sat and pondered for long nights until the fires burned low and the sun came up; only then could i sleep in its warmth.

My heart wanted to tread all the land and breathe the air of the high snow-capped mountains. Feeling the rawness of nature has always been one of my favorite passions; standing on a precipice or a cliff, high above the river, a strong wind blowing in my face and hair. Rain, thunder chasing after the lightning in the forest at night. Sometimes I would track bears in the woods, watching them from far off making sure to not be seen. I would often come across track dilemmas that I could not identify, so I would draw them and ask other older, more wiser woodsmen. Sometimes even they would just scratch their heads in wonderment or disbelief; all these things I pondered.

Having been told to never return was clashing with the plea of the wood-folk for their help in my groggy head in the early light: one a desperate plea to rid the creature from the mine, the other a cold hard death threat. The stones that I bore in the wood chest I hoped would be enticing to the kings. The elders gave them to me at great cost to them as a down payment for a service their very lives depended upon—and mine as well. There were a score of men already killed by the dark spawn that had taken over the mine of the wood-folk, and more maimed or mad with fear. There must be an answer to this dilemma; fire was this thing's fiend and a weapon that it could wield.

As my thoughts moved back and forth between my ears, I saw that when the crystal in my new found staff was moved into the darkest of the cliff overhang that it had a faint glow, a slight radiation not a reflection. It was a two-sun march from the wood-folk's dwellings from this high mountain pass. I sat hoping to hear something that would give me an idea about the problems away down below. The songs inside the wall went on and on through the night. These people must sleep during the sunlight. As I listened, I kept looking for a passageway or a crawl space; the music inside the mountain called out to me.

The way down to the river from the north was a Gentle slope as if worn by great boulders and stones rolled down to the water from the ridge above. The river was deep and wide in that place. From above, I could see no place to cross; the current was moving fast. Once to the edge, I could see large stones just below the surface like an underwater bridge, as I stepped out on them the pressure almost swept me away, so I found a large rock in a pile of others and added its weight to mine as I stood on the first stone, feeling the rush of cold water as it climbed up my legs and soaked me to the skin. And so I went from stone to stone toward the southern shore and the crumbled bulkhead of the dark inner palace of the twin scaly creatures. I could hear that hissing voice almost as if it was yesterday: "Do not return to us".

I was met on the other shore of the river by the dragon with the two yellow eyes, he was tearing and pacing the ground, very agitated and upset he was... He ducked his head low toward me as he spoke; the heat of his breath almost turned me inside out. "I knew of your coming and would not wait inside, you seem wise beyond your years to leave the horse and wolf behind in the trees of the far ridge. Wait for me as I survey the land about; go in and dry by the fire." Before I could ask about his brother, the elegant lizard leapt for the sky and soared away like a feather in the wind. Again, I moved into the stone stronghold listening and watching for the one green eyed sibling. It wasn't long before I could tell that things were not right, even for this torched place. First off, the bad smell had risen to a stench and the blue gem that sat before the thrones was missing from its perch. In the dimness, I could see the shadowed outline of the other dragon sprawled along the back wall, the headless and rank mass of the other winged monarch kept me back from moving in closer to inspect the damage done. Just then, the other dragon scrambled in with Thunder and the wolf in tow. I just could not imagine how he did that; they both were calm almost sleepy, just the opposite of the dragon who was writhing in non-ending movement, never stopping as he spoke, "You were long getting here man-ling and what is it we called you?" He paused long, looking at his dead brother as if for the first time the way it is now. "We... The Rover, yes, you are the Rover," the lizard kept moving with furtive glances around as if it would never be calm again. "The fire creature came from deep within the fortress seven or eight nights back it took the jewel and killed us; we wounded it to the bone and it went back into the darkness; followed it; yes but could not keep its trail... never have we seen a creature borne of fire that we could not track or kill. Today I leave for a high mountain loft that we had many seasons ago. There I will consider for some time the plea that you bring from the wood-folk for it seems we seek after the same end. I also know about the chest of stones your steed caries to pay us for help; that you may keep. The large blue stone we call the river stone, if it can be found is yours as well. I only want the hide of that beast when you run him down. Me? You think I can do what the dragon kings of the river cannot...You sir give great credit above my prowess. Even if I could track it back into the darkness, then what would I do? Turning back on itself, the great dragon pulled from a missing place in its scales a leather bag— dragon leather. "This is the blood of my brother. Now, having been slain by the creature it will in turn kill him if it touches him in the least bit. That stone in your staff will grow brighter as you go deeper into darkness and guide your manling eyes. And the scent of fire can be followed by the wolf, where I could not. I am away to the high places." And so, he was. I relieved the other dragon of his claws and teeth knowing they would be of know more use to him. Thunder began to sniff and glare sideways at the clutch of dragon parts I put into the message bag. I wondered if I would be able to get him to go back into the foul-smelling darkness at all. I tied the message bag on the back of Thunder and kept the vial of dragon blood with me in a fold of my cloak. The horse did not mind the strange burden. I lifted my staff, and we moved off into the embrace of the receding gloom.

There it was again.... as a peal of thunder in a clear blue sky. I remember one time This same Voice woke me from a sound sleep. The voice told me ... (it was more of a suggestion than an order or decree) to break camp and double back up to an eastern ridge and to await the sunrise. From that vantage point, I could see fell creatures slink up upon the place of my old camp, moving like shadows, sniffing the ground, crawling and squirming on my scent. Had it not been for the waking of the inner voice and my listening to it, there is no telling what dread would have come of that morn. When the sun did hit the camp, they scattered like the morning mist. Another time, the voice spoke to me slow and clear: "Do not take that path."

Simple enough; there were at least two other well-worn and traveled roads to my destination, so I picked the first one that came to mind. A few days later, I found out that on the path that the voice warned me about a bridge had been carried away by the river; I would have lost many days' travel and valuable information needed could have been waylaid.

So now, here in the dark tunnel of the cave deep in the mountain, with only the light of my staff and its reflection in the eyes of my friends, I heard the voice and I took heed. I stopped and went to one knee, Woulph turned back to me and sat.

Thunder, my steed, had grown accustomed to the low light and nuzzled my arm, not out of fear or Impatience but his compassion and playfulness. We had been in the tunnels for three turns of the sun into the next moon. We had fresh water that we drank from clear pools, and we ate fish that massed within them. Strange fish with milky sightless eyes yet tasty even raw. Listening, waiting. The voice of direction; this is how I had begun to trust in it…. "Put the light in your staff out and sit for a while in the dark." At first, thunder got a little edgy, then settled down, Woulph paced a while then laid beside me and slept. Over the past three turns of the sundown in this darkness, I had left the light of my staff on as much for vision as to ward off anything we did not or could not see. As my eyes tried to adjust to the complete darkness around us, I became aware of a faint glow before us... reddish. Woulph's ears went up and he sniffed the air, in the quietness it was as loud as a howl in the open fields. Thunder stood as a stone, not so much as a twitch. The reddish light got slowly brighter and brighter. I had no doubt that the creature was before us, moving in our direction. I began to make preparation for its death, Woulph stayed low and moved not. I felt around in the red glow, silently moving things around packs and sacks, I could feel a surge building in me. When all was ready, there were breathing sounds now and scraping, we could feel the heat as the light of its approach grew in the darkness. The thing was still several turns up the cavern away from our view. Woulph was now standing at full alert by my side, and thunder was casting hopeful glances back down the way we had come. I had learned to master the stone in my staff while in this darkness. flashing it like blue lightning and dropping it down to the gentle glow of a firefly and then to its cold stone rest that it was now. My plan was to blast it at the creature just before I struck him with the blood of the river king, ending its life and dreadful fire forever. The dark forces that drove the creature were long forgotten. The stone that it clung to as if for its very life was, in fact, why the creature was created so very long ago—to steal it and others like it, to guard it for his master in his lust for power and dominance over all things pure and evil. Only the dragon had a small idea of the value of the stone and the age of its curse or the evil that drove the beast. Now only one of the kings remained, and he had flown for safety above and beyond the home of the eagles, leaving the stone to fate in the hands of a young wizard, if that is what I was. Long ago, even as dragons count time, the river had brought the stone to the front of the castle in a storm. A storm so powerful that the river had run backward from the sea tides for nine turns of the sun. Saltwater went into lakes and brought all kinds of strange things, but the strangest by far was the stone left on the threshold of the fortress. Together, the kings rolled it inside and hid it; searching and searching to find its origin in old scrolls, but all was lost of its tale save only a rumor of a lustful evil that would stop at nothing, even time to obtain it, killing all in its way. Knowing this, the brothers kept it in their hoard as a show of prowess and strength that lead to their recent demise. The stone gave off a blue light and burned the creature to its core.

Only fear of a greater pain kept it in its claws. The size of the stone was like a small loaf of bread, built with a craft and beauty never before seen this side of the western sea. All this was lost on the creature, who was only bent on his pursuers and the burning pain the trinket gave him. I put my hand on the wall of the cave, feeling the rough-hewn stone trying to calm my nerves my other hand on Woulph's head, the vial down at my feet ready for my next move. My staff was leaning against the wall, everything was ready except for Thunder. Just then, as the creature came around the corner, Thunder made such a racket that it sent the plan of surprise to splinters. I looked over my shoulder, and all I could see was four hooves and a tail moving fast down the tunnel away into the darkness. Woulph looked both ways in a manner that made me laugh. He could not decide whether to guard me against this menacing peril or to corral up the wayward horse... the whole thing had me laughing and rolling on the floor of the cave, forgetting my fear in a moment of mindless overwhelming joy. There stood the fire creature, hunched over staring at me, stunned by the actions that were oblivious to him. I did not even glance in his direction until it was too late. I raised my staff with a blinding flash and with an underhand shot, hit him full in the chest. The dragon spoke the truth, and the light of its fire went dim and then out like a winter sunset in the face of a storm; just a falling pile like dry straw from the back of a wagon, no thrashing or screaming. Woulph ran down the dark expanse, making his mind up to collect Thunder and return him to me. All I could do was laugh at the irony of the clapping of Thunder's hooves before the strike of my lightning; sitting in the now brightly lit and quiet

Thünder

The Stone Cave

Down, down, down the steeply winding way we went, the angle of decent made for slow careful footing. All along the way, I was aware of the smoothness of the floor and walls overhead were more polished than hewn, no runes or markings to guide or suggest what lay ahead or behind. So, on we plodded till the way became lit from up ahead in the light we would find our way. I looked back at Thunder and the team of ponies to see that their ears were forward, and they were gulping in the freshening air; Woulph went up ahead he would do this often to check the trail, our spirits were greatly lifted at the aspect of coming to the end of the tunnel. Soon, it opened up into a large cavern filled with multiple-colored stones; crystals that would glow on their own accord, some would spark up and others would return a spark as if answering in reply we stopped for a while and took it all in with joy and amazement. However, our need for fresh air and the great blue sky overcame us, and we moved on to the cave opening. What I took for bird calls quickly turned to sounds made by the elven guards set about the cave entrance outside.

We never saw them until they had us surrounded in a small glen; bows taught, and arrows notched. No one spoke or moved. Slowly, one by one, all eyes turned to the dead and skinned fire delver flung over Thunders back, weapons lowered, and words were spoken slow and low. Our small party was still overwhelmed by the light, blinded by the truth that we were now outside of the darkness and walking in the light and in that light, we would find the road.

Usually, I am not one to remember my dreams if I have them; but with the dark nights sleeping in the tunnel, I would awaken to dark thoughts—too dark to be my own. It was like some malevolent force had been slipping them into my normally peaceful composed mind. Painfully torched images that I would later have to expel in the morning light. My conclusion was that everybody needs the light and that no matter how dark the night, life and love return to the soul in the light. My thoughts began to clear and the wind was refreshing me even in the midst of our captors, I began to smile and yes, even laugh knowing we had reached Witt's people. The way of it was that no matter how disillusioned the elves were concerning our emergence of the cave, we were out of it. I began to laugh out loud in the reality of how our exit was their entrance as I stood there with a clear perspective that we had gone out through the in-door. Elves and dwarfs do not think in the same terms, and their methods of merrymaking differ greatly, but the same crucial ingredients remain the same: song, dance, and ale. This camp of elves were of different concepts; some drank way more than they danced or sang, and others played on instruments, sang, danced, and hardly drank at all. So the heavy drinkers turned in early while the singers went on till sunrise, even some till mid-morn. All through the night, the melody followed currents and eddies along a river of tunes, but its song remained the same. Banners flapped fluidly in the wind, reminding me of the flying skirts and dresses of the dancing she-elves from the prior eve, but mostly it reminded me of Witt, twirling and floating. My eyes hardly left her.

We danced together long into the night. Low clouds began to skim over the mountaintops above us, racing away east.

The elfin warriors stood in ranks as an army prepared for war. Their commander spoke in a dialect I did not understand. Before him, laid out on a field table, was the hide of the fire delver, and on the ground before it was the chest of stones that had made the round trip. I made a point to return the stones knowing that the payment was for the river kings to bring destruction on the beast, after all I still had the blue stone that I would not surrender to dwarf or elf. Witt as the other elves began to look at me in another light; not that of leery mistrust, but in a type of expectation of what I might do or say next. I had told my story around the fire to all who would listen, of how destruction came to the beast. I sat with the elders of this gentle race as Elfin masters raised their cups and sang songs in words I could not yet comprehend; but joy was in the telling, as comfort came from the creatures felling.

The cave was now free again, and its trade was flowing in all directions. Two riders were approaching with Harold's before and behind on foot. They were barring the cask of jewels and presented them to me along with a fine sheathed sword and a robe of stately appearance, this was draped over my shoulder likewise the sword handed to me unsheathing it the barer knelt, sunlight glinted blue and green, glimmering off its superlative steel. The elves not to be outdone by dwarves in any measure, gave to me also a shield and a great white stead that had never been saddled or bridled. The steed many hands taller than any horse I had ever seen or heard of by its appearance and barring alone was a gift suitable for a king. After this ceremony, conducted with no small heraldry, I was taken to a dwelling and told it was mine. It was laid out in an orchard, away up the hill and back down the other side to a spring-fed creek flowing away to the south. There I stowed my many fortunes and plunder with the white steed and Thunder loose in the fields, Woulph by my side, I slept in a chair by the fire that night, with Witt tucked under my shoulder. With My boots by the door and my swords hung with pride on the wall, a completeness filled my heart... that day Witt agreed to be my wife. We both wanted this to last forever, knowing none of this was possible and that just made the wonder and beauty of the moment so much more the real treasure to us. I gladly gave the jewels to Witt's kinfolk for her hand, even after they first refused. I had Witt and her sister help me slide them to the foot of their bed. Witt's sister had unlatched the door from the inside and ever so quietly, we placed them with my new shield leaning over it. The emblem on the shield was a symbol of the highest house among the wood folk, and none could argue against its wish or word even in the great councils threw out the land, for so much sway it held. Long sweet days and blissful nights we enjoyed for many turns of the moon. A wanderer came from the lower lands. His news was grievous and bitter with pain. The yellow eyes of the night had returned. These dark dwellers had many names, none of them as nasty as their vile reputation.

The woodlanders called them yellow eyes because wholesome folks' eyes were clear, bright, and did not shine back in the night like a beast. Their eyes would shine yellow in the dark and were a pale dull yellow in the daylight. For half an age, there was no news or sightings of them. My thoughts were that it was the fire delver himself that had kept them at bay for so long. So great was its wrath, fear of Him kept the yellow eyes out of the tunnels and far to the southeast. Now, with him gone, they began to harry folk all along the rim of the mountains. War was in the wind.

This morning my mind took me back to a place filled with danger I had been aware of the cats for some time, huge they were, and very elusive; it was rare to even see one out in the open. I would sometimes catch glimpses of them darting and jumping away up steep embankments or into the deep darkness of a tree line; I would see their tracks along the river sides where they would stop to drink water and then vanish away with small traces Sometimes, I would hear them cry out with the lonely sound they made like a lost baby. Today

Fire
Delver

as I sat on the ridge I could see one..... It had a horse or a large pony grasped behind its two great front top teeth the legs of its prey slightly dragging as it trotted across a low grassy field I used my staff to see it up close. I found that I could use the crystal in my staff to enlarge Things to my eye and see far-off things as if they were closer by turning it to just the right angles; I could also light fires from it in the daytime letting the sunshine threw another angle I kept finding more and more uses for such an old stick. Thunder was chomping grass away off to my side he did not see the cat with its clutch. woulph began to sniff the air behind me and then growl, snapping and snarling he maneuvered in to protect me at that moment another cat leaped over us without as much as a glance as it ran headlong down the side of the mountain toward the other cat. I had rolled away pulling my sword I grabbed the main of thunder to hold him less he bolts away in fear; things can happen and sometimes do that can strip you of everything and leave you with only your cloak and that is what happens when your horse bolts with everything you own. The cats far below merged as one rolling and scrapping. The largest one the one that had leapt over us sent the other cat away while stealing its prize.

Thunder, Woulph and I were sitting there on the ridge trying to regain some kind of composure I was feeling very grateful that the big cat had other ideas for its meal than us. None of us had any knowledge of the big cat being that close by when it leaped, only Woulph gave any warning before it sprang; we had calmed ourselves and I was watching through my staff stone, the big cat finish what he wanted and head into the woods. The sun was at third watch, over a tree line I saw what at first looked like a group of eagles surveying the carnage slowly they circled down to land on the horse carcass. These birds were large but not as large as an eagle, they began to tear and rip at the flesh fighting amongst each other in some structured contest of power and craftiness. Again, I heard the voice I began referring to as the voice of the creator based on the way he knew things worked and interacted as they concerned my life.

The creator spoke: "These birds are vultures and like the eagle, they use the thermals of the winds like currents in a river. As the eagle spirals up and upon them the vulture spins down on the smell of death, both the eagle and the vulture were omens one for awareness and the other for danger." I tried not to shutter at my smallness and vulnerability in this vast world. Things just got bigger as my awareness grew of my part in it; I could hear it calling me back to my home... In the days of my youth, I was told what it means to be a man; now I've reached that age to try and do those things the best I can. It was as the beating of my heart; a rhyme like the rhythm of life itself.

Once, there was a time such as this that in the distance, out on a moonlit plain, I saw a giant of a man change into a bear and walk off into the woods. Strange things walked this world, so great care must be given to those you love to protect them and teach them wisdom and, in turn, listen and learn even more. This is how I felt about my friends Thunder and Woulph, and not the least to Witt would my thoughts often go always wishing her well; and something more. It was thoughts of her that warmed me at night and kept me cool in the midday sun. From the day of the first Harold all sorts of peoples and stories came up from the South; Homes and fields set ablaze, entire villages destroyed over night like a black tide came the hoards of the amber eyed nightmare. Scouts began to report the extent of the migration and sheer masses of the swarms staggering number told us that this was no small infiltration or expanded meandering ... This was a full-scale invasion. The elves were Quick to rally full armies. It was at this time that I went to warn and enlist the help of the dwarfs. With the combination of the two peoples, some chance of defense could be made. If we were left to fight Un aided both elves and dwarfs faced imminent destruction. So, I went through the cave on the morning of the next day. After a long embrace in witch time Witt showed great courage, she did not sob or sigh I told her I would return to her, with her burning green eyes Witt looked deep into mine as she held my face in her hands she said since I've been loving you, I have learned to trust your council and I will stay within the fortifications and await your return. I left Thunder with her; Woulph and I rode off me on the white steed flying an elvish banner of the king. We came across no resistance or sign of the fell creatures. It was slow going up and up the slope, leading the steed, following Woulph who always loped ahead to spy the tunnels before us. As we got closer, I could hear Woulph growling far up the tunnel he did not return I lowered the light on my staff and drew my sword. When I rounded the opening to the great hall of the dwarf lords under the mountains It was plain to see a great battle had been fought in this place. To count the dead would stager the mind of any man, elf or dwarf. A large contingency of the dwarf army had survived by building an inner stone barricade to stem the onslaught of their attackers of which there was no living sign. The horrific piles of the fallen told the tale of fifteen to one as the dwarfs dealt out their deadly axe and sword blows leaving no quarter. The yellow eyes were strewn everywhere and there had not been time for the dwarfs to retrieve their fallen.

I must have arrived just as the last attack had been held off. They had come through the very spot broken in the wall that our small party came through last spring. There was no time for sorrow or mourning, only a cry to arms and to redouble the guard and prepare for the next wave if that was to be our lot. I led the steed to the elders and presented my plan: to band together with the wood folk and hunt down the rest of the dark-lings, and find out what beyond their own rage, drove them on it seemed that a darker mind loomed behind them, shaping their brutish wrath to its will. This time I left the hall of the dwarfs by way of their main gate, it was then that Woulph rejoined me. I was stricken by the outside air even the wind was fouled by some tainted evil blowing up from the South. This time of season usually the wind was blowing from the West, fresh and clear bringing hope for a long harvest. This wind was foreboding, dark and rank, suffocating the hearts of men, dwarf and elf alike. The sun with its warmth felt far off leaving a chill to the bone. My new white steed was wrestles; weary from the smell of death and carnage so I healed him on to the top

of a rise hoping for a better vantage point, perhaps a bit cheery of a view. The scene from the top was dismal and gloomy; The horizon was smoldering from fires set in the place of homes and villages. Even the river was chocked with wreckage, ash and burnt timbers the cries of low-flying crows filled the air like a lament. I resolved in my heart to stop this rush of evil by any means. there was a hush on the land with out a foe in sight It was like the peaceful rest between the fire of the forge and the anvil as the steal is shaped by the hammer of the gods. High on the misty tops of the mountains away to the North the dark wind did not reach the smoke was only visible to the eagles high in their lofts. There was a gathering of the regal creatures from far and wide most of them bringing reports of fear of what was and what should never be; feathers were preened, and war was in the air. The eagles could hear the voices crying down in the valleys below. Men drawn from their farms and the woods, strong men with great resolve, men who had come to put an end to this plague. Long-standing grudges were left off in place of a fresh unity; wagons loaded with weapons and provisions came from afar. Armies from the North came down the old road. Stern men bold and valiant; hardened by long wars with enemies from the East. New defenses went up and scouts sent to all corners of the land to spy out the foe.

DARK SPIRE

There was a dark malevolence behind this surge of black tide, a whirlwind of hatred for all things good and fair in the land. His name if he had one would change as it did in every age; A shadow only a wisp of who he was created to be, once glorious to behold beautiful of speech but now only a dark wraith of vengeance wielding fear as a weapon of power. Those who walked a fearless path took slight notice of him safe to laugh at his foolishness. Alas but these were times of fear and the fearless were a rare bread upon the land; there were a few and the Darkness knew of them he could however not manipulate them with his fear, so he gave them no to little heed. The fearless did not know each other or for that matter, they did know that they were fearless or few. One thing the few held common was the knowledge that truth is light and in light there is no darkness or shadow of turning so fear in and of itself has no substance to be afraid of .... like a void in darkest night a cloak of formlessness in its rebelliousness it wanted to destroy even itself. It was loathing of all living things especially those that were close to the light. were did such a creature hide not any place I ever wanted to venture unless... I had to: a shudder went through me, and I decided to change my thoughts from such dark musings.

I sent my thoughts away toward the north to my sweet witt, to the Rudy velvet strength she always walked in; her memory blew threw my mind like a gentle summer breeze sending all the pain away like cobwebs before a flame. All my hope was in a brighter day, as warm spring rain to wash all this away. Things were quiet as the sun went down on a day of sadness.

Over the hills, far away behind the gates of the hidden elvish stronghold high in the mountains the news of the losses came trickling in. Witt fought hard her urge to saddle thunder and ride to the south and be by her man a dangerous idea a task she was up to but then wisdom prevailed in her heart, so she remained in the safety of the stronghold. It was time for me to turn my face to the north and report back to the king of the wood-folk. It was agreed upon by the dwarfs to rekindle the old alliance and join together against the yellow eyes. Long after the darkness of the night set in the children of the sun began to awake and dance in the dark of night; sing to the morning light. Long gliding steps made by the white steed, purposeful in rhythm it kept my mind like a cadence; hooves after hove soothing my heart and distracting me from pain. The movements of the steed had a timeless wisdom that ran threw its veins even now it seemed to sense my thoughts. I stayed my tears for the fallen adding their bitterness to my task. The air began to refresh me the wind slapping the king's banner in time with the white steed's canter. there was an evil on this southern wind; turning the very nature of things twisted into a madness that had taken the minds of the wolfs. The clans that for long years respected each other's domain by the law of the fang and claw they had kept to their own by means of hunting and sprawling to the size of their individual needs. The drastic change was that they had begun to pack together by legions and moving against menfolk and their livestock. News of this came hard to me, Woulph was always loyal and kind in his way from the time he was a pup. The men began to watch him in a nervous way keeping their distance and speaking in low tones around us. So far the madness had not effected him he did however become aware of the different way the others began to act around him. Woulph was large and muscular for his breed at least two hands taller than any other and along with his bright coat and blue eyes he would stand out any ware amongst other wolf; there was also a war harness that he wore in the colors of the elf king....up ahead I saw an open ended lodge were some of the elf scouts had built a fire to get out of the cold. The southern wind cut. and they spoke little giving Woulph and I a place of honor next to the hearth. The sound of there melodic voices as they spoke the old toung of their people felt like home. The Warmth of the fire was a welcome friend even its smoke was cleaner than the outside air. Woulph slept at my side as the chill was lifted from us; my heart was made a little bit lighter I had to fight to keep my thoughts from the grim void that our world had become. again, the heart of my love called to me from the halls of the elf king in my thoughts I could see rings of smoke threw the trees and hear the voices of those who came looking. I drew solace from the deep glow of the embers, reaching for the pool of peace within me I sat starring at the fire before me; all the sounds and movements around me slowly faded to a far-off hum like wind through trees somehow, I knew that together we would defeat this foe no matter how ancient no matter how foul.

This concludes the first scroll of memories that filtered down through the stars across the sun under the moon between the clouds into my mind drawn by my hand for those who can hear......

www.ingramcontent.com/pod-product-compliance
Lightning Source LLC
Chambersburg PA
CBHW042050010826
48978CB00023B/1341